Characters

Billy Taylor a new boy at school
Mrs Taylor Billy's mum

Millie
Jasmine
Humza ⎱ pupils at the school
Raki
Ishrak

Miss Philips a teacher
Mr Sweet the head teacher
Mr Flinton a teacher who runs the school football team

The Pharaoh the king of Egypt
The High Priest
The Vizier the prime minister of Egypt

Meti
Ebio ⎱ mummies

Baker an Egyptian baker
Sabola the baker's son
Mummy 1
Mummy 2
Messenger the pharaoh's messenger
Other mummies

The first children to act Millie were Hana Ayers and Georgia Salisbury. The first to be Billy were Macaulay Whistler and Oliver Long.

The Pharaoh's Toothache
Act One Scene One

Billy is walking to his new school with his mother

Mrs Taylor: You'll be all right, won't you Billy?

Billy: Mum, stop fussing.

Mrs Taylor: Have you got your lunchbox?

Billy: Yep.

Mrs Taylor: What about your PE kit?

Billy: I won't need it on the first day of term.

Mrs Taylor: How do you know? I put it out for you. Don't you like PE?

Billy: PE is fine, Mum. Please don't make a fuss.

Mrs Taylor: There's nothing wrong with a bit of exercise, Billy.

Billy: I know, so why don't you go to the gym instead of nagging me then?

Mrs Taylor: There's no need to be cheeky, Billy. You're bound to feel a bit nervous on your first day at a new school.

4

Billy: Yep, sorry Mum. But you don't have to come in. I'll be fine.

(Children enter in a group – Jasmine, Humza, Raki, Ishrak and Millie. They are looking at something Millie is holding)

Mrs Taylor: Look, there's some of the other children. Are you going to say hello?

Children: Sssssssssssssssssssssssssssssssssssss.

Mrs Taylor: Goodness me, has that girl got a snake?

Jasmine: It's Millie with her pet snake. She's going to show it to the class. Come and have a look!

Mrs Taylor: No thank you. I'll leave you here, I'm sure you'll be fine now you've made some friends. Kiss, kiss!

(Billy reluctantly kisses his mother on the cheek. She hurries away)

Billy: Bye, Mum, see you later. Have a good time at the gym!

Mrs Taylor: What? Oh yes, very funny. Have a nice day, love. *(Exits)*

Humza: Are you the new kid?

Billy: Yes.

Humza: Come and see
Millie's snake.

Billy: Er, no thanks.

Raki: It won't hurt you! Well, only if it bites you!

(The other children laugh)

Jasmine: Are you scared?

Billy: No. Well, a bit. Anyway I think I'm supposed to go to the head teacher.

Raki: I'll take you. It's this way.

Humza: Hey Millie, that new kid is scared of your snake!

(The other children follow Millie into the playground while Raki takes Billy into school)

Scene Two

Inside the school

Raki: He's OK really, is Sweetie, but he doesn't always listen to what we say – I suppose he's got a lot on his mind.

Billy: Who's Sweetie?

Raki: The Head. But don't call him that. Here he is.

(They meet Mr Sweet)

Mr Sweet: Where is it? Where's it gone?

Raki: Er, Mr Sweet?

Mr Sweet: I definitely left it here and now it's gone. Why does everything keep disappearing in this school?

Raki: Mr Sweet, this is the new boy.

Mr Sweet: Oh, right. Thank you, Raki. You can go.

(Raki leaves)

Hello, I'm Mr Sweet and I'm the head teacher. Isn't your mum with you?

Billy: No, she had to go.

Mr Sweet: I'm sorry, I did look up your name but there's been so much going on…

Billy: Billy. Billy Taylor.

Mr Sweet: You didn't see anyone carrying chocolate on your way in, did you? One of the children, or the staff? Or the people in the office?

Billy: No.

Mr Sweet: Right, I just thought I'd ask. So tell me about yourself, Billy. What do you like to do? Do you like football?

Billy: Yes, I play in goal. Have you got a school team?

Mr Sweet: Yes, Mr Flinton runs it. You'll see him in assembly. That's great, we need a goalie. And what else do you like to do?

Billy: I like reading.

Mr Sweet: Really? That's marvelous.

(Children make a noise just outside the window)

What's all this? *(He opens the window)* Come here, Millie, and go to your classes, the rest of you.

(Millie comes in. She is holding something up her sleeve)

What's going on out there, Millie?

Millie: I was just showing them Sid.

Mr Sweet: Sid? Is that another new boy? I thought there was only one starting today.

Millie: Sid is my snake. Miss Philips said I could bring him in for show and tell.

Mr Sweet: Did she? I shall be having words with that Miss Philips today, if I can find her. Sometimes she seems to disappear into thin air. Now, where was I? Oh yes: Millie, this is Billy.

Millie: Hiya. Say hello to Sid.

Billy: Is he real?

Millie: Why, are you scared?

Mr Sweet: Calm down, Millie. You'll be glad to know that Billy is a goalkeeper.

Millie: Are you any good?

Billy: Not bad, I reckon.

Millie: Catch this! *(She flicks Sid the snake at Billy, who jumps back. Millie has kept hold of Sid's tail and pulls him back up her sleeve)*

Mr Sweet: That's enough, Millie. I want you to take Billy to your class and make sure he settles in.

Millie: OK, Mr Sweet. I'll take care of him.

Scene Three

Millie and Billy leave the head teacher's office and talk as they go through the hall to the classroom

Millie: Are you scared of Sid?

Billy: I'm not used to snakes. Is he real? It's hard to tell.

(Ishrak enters and sees Millie and Billy)

Millie: Hang on a sec. *(She stops by the music system and changes the music CD in the machine)* That should liven up the assembly.

Ishrak: What are you doing, Millie?

Millie: None of your business, Ishrak.

Ishrak: You're not supposed to touch the CDs. I'll tell.

Millie: Stand still a sec, Ishrak. *(She takes Sid from her sleeve and swings him to and fro in front of Ishrak)* Watch the snake. Watch the snake. You are feeling sleepy. When you wake up, you won't remember me changing the CD. *(She snaps her fingers. Ishrak wakes up)*

Ishrak: Hi Millie.

Millie: Hiya Ishrak. What are you up to?

10

Ishrak: I'm getting the register. See you later! *(Exits)*

Billy: Did you really hypnotise that kid?

Millie: Cool, isn't it?

Billy: So that's not a real snake?

Millie: You ARE scared of Sid, aren't you? What a wimp!

Billy: Well, I'm scared if he's real. He looks like he might be one of those wooden ones, but I can't tell.

Millie: Would you like to hold him?

Billy: Um, aren't we late for class now?

Millie: I thought so. You're scared. Come on, Mister Scared New Boy.

(They enter the classroom)

Scene Four

The class are colouring maps of Egypt

Miss Philips: So, we've found out how important the River Nile was in Ancient Egypt. Who can tell us something about it?

(Billy puts his hand up)

Yes, Billy?

Billy: The wind pushed the sailboats one way, and the
current took them the other way, so it was easy
to travel up and down on it.

Miss Philips: Well done, Billy. We hadn't talked about that, how did you know?

Billy: I read it in a book.

Miss Philips: That is a good example to the whole class, Billy. Well done.

Millie: *(Quietly)* Not bad for a scaredy-cat.

Miss Philips: What was that, Millie?

Millie: Nothing, Miss. When can I show my snake?

Miss Philips: Later. Millie, I would like you and Billy to stay behind while the rest of the class goes to the temple.

Jasmine: The temple, Miss?

Miss Philips: Oh, silly me, no. Assembly. Off you go to assembly, everyone.

(The class exits apart from Millie and Billy. Miss Philips takes some chocolate from her pocket as she talks)

Miss Philips: Now, Millie, I think you have something you need to say to Billy.

Millie: No I don't. He's a wimp.

Billy: No I'm not.

Millie: You are, 'cos you're scared of Sid.

Billy: Only if he's real.

Miss Philips: Now now, this is all a waste of time. Millie, what do I do with children who aren't getting on?

Millie: Oh, no, Miss, don't give us a job to do together. Please! Just let me go to the assembly.

(Loud rock music suddenly blasts out from the hall. It stops abruptly and is replaced by the sound of Mr Sweet shouting angrily)

Miss Philips: Hmm. Sounds like someone has played a practical joke with the music in the hall. That's just the sort of thing you do, Millie. Shall I send you to Mr Sweet now?

Millie: Er, no thanks, Miss Philips. Perhaps I could do a job with Billy?

Billy: Who's the scaredy-cat now, then?

Miss Philips: That's enough, you two. Now, I want you to pack all the colouring pencils in this box, and I am putting you both in charge of our Ancient Egypt display. Please keep it tidy. You'll need to sweep the sand towards the little pyramid if it gets scattered but – and this is very important – you must never, ever, rub this scarab.

Millie: What's a scarab?

Billy: It's that thing that looks like a beetle. They were good luck charms in Ancient Egypt.

Millie: What a know-it-all you are!

Miss Philips: That's enough, Millie. Just remember, never rub that scarab. Just leave it alone. Now give me the box of pencils and go to assembly.

(Billy and Millie leave one way, and Miss Philips quickly disappears another way. Before they reach the door, Millie suddenly stops)

Millie: Hang on, where's Sid?

Billy: Is this another one of your practical jokes?

Millie: No, honestly, I can't find him. Miss Philips, have you seen Sid?

Billy: She's gone! She was right there a moment ago, and now she's not.

Millie: She must have gone for a coffee. Oh, here's Sid – he was up my arm all the time!

(Mr Flinton walks in)

Mr Flinton: Come on you two, you should be in assembly. Get a move on!

(Exit)

Scene Five

Millie and Billy creep into the assembly, followed by Mr Flinton

Mr Sweet: … so if anyone knows who changed the assembly music, I'd like to hear from them.

(Ishrak puts his hand up. Billy and Millie exchange a worried look)

Yes, Ishrak?

Ishrak: Um, er, I've forgotten, Mr Sweet.

Millie: *(Very quietly)* Phew, that was close.

Mr Sweet: Hmm. Well at least the other CD was still here. You may have noticed that equipment is disappearing from the school. Ah, Mr Flinton, is there any sign of those new blue football tops?

Mr Flinton: None, Mr Sweet. They've all gone. One minute they were in the PE store, the next they weren't. It's very strange.

Mr Sweet: We've lost boxes of pencils, rulers, rubbers. A whole set of desks disappeared last week and now this football kit has gone. Does anybody know anything about it?

(Ishrak puts his hand up)

Yes, Ishrak?

Ishrak: Um… Er… I've forgotten.

Mr Sweet: That's the second time you've put your hand up and forgotten what you were going to say. Are you losing your mind, Ishrak?

Ishrak: Sorry, Mr Sweet.

Mr Sweet: Now, what was I saying? Ah yes, things disappearing. We need money, so we're going to have a fancy dress day tomorrow, where you can wear anything you like.

Children: Hurray!

Mr Sweet: But you have to bring in some money. We'll use it to pay for all the equipment which has been taken. The last straw was this morning. A bar of chocolate was taken from my desk!

Children: GASP!

Mr Sweet: I cannot possibly be expected to run the school without having my chocolate at break times. So if I can't face my break time, you won't get one either. Until that chocolate is returned, there will be no break times at all.

Children: Oh no!

Millie: *(Whispering under the groans)* Hey Billy, I think I know who took that chocolate: it was Miss Philips. Do you remember she was eating it while she told us about the display?

Billy: Oh yes, she was. And she put it down by the scarab!

Millie: We've got to get it back or there will be no break times, and we won't get to play football. Follow me.

(They crawl out of assembly, going under Mr Flinton's chair while he is trying to get the complaining children to calm down)

Scene Six

By the classroom display

Millie: Here's the scarab. It's been moved. But where's the chocolate?

Billy: Let's have a look under these books. Ooops! *(He knocks all the books across the display)*

Millie: You nit! Look what you've done. It's a right mess, and the sand is all over the display!

Billy: Don't be such a fusspot: you're worse than my mum. It's OK, I'll tidy it up. It just needs a quick wipe.

*(There is a rumbling sound and Millie and Billy
scream as they are pulled out through the wall)*

Act Two Scene One

Millie and Billy find themselves in a cloud of sand. It slowly clears during the scene to reveal they are in a temple near a pyramid, in Ancient Egypt

Millie: I can't see, my eyes are full of sand.

Billy: Me too. Just stay still and keep blinking. I think part of the school has fallen down. They'll come and help us soon.

Millie: Are you OK?

Billy: I didn't think you cared.

Millie: Well I asked, didn't I?

Billy: Yep. Sorry. I'm fine, just a bit dusty. But it's out of my eyes now. WOW!

Millie: What? Has the whole school fallen down?

Billy: That's a pyramid.

Millie: What, the little one in the display? I'll get it. Yuk, your hand is all slimy!

Billy: That's not my hand. It's a camel's tongue!

Millie: Get off me, you slimy camel. I've got a snake! *(The camel runs away)* Hang on, Billy, we're not

in school, are we? Sand, pyramids, camels: we're in Egypt!

Billy: I don't know how but yes, we are.

Millie: Shh! I can hear voices!

(The High Priest and the Vizier enter)

High Priest: So we're agreed, then, Vizier?

Vizier: As long as you keep your side of the bargain, yes.

High Priest: Oh you can trust me. After all, I talk with the gods.

Vizier: But our plan must be kept secret. Don't even mention it to the gods.

High Priest: Do you take me for a fool? Even my army does not know what I intend to do.

Vizier: Good. Now I must go back to the palace. The pharaoh will be expecting me. *(Exits)*

High Priest: Yes, off you go, you silly man. I'll get rid of you as soon as I'm in charge.

(Billy slips and falls over with a crash)

Who's there? Come out immediately!

Millie: Blimey, he sounds like Mr Sweet on a bad day when all the chocolate has run out. Let's run the other way!

(A mummy enters)

Billy: Mummy! A mummy!

Millie: This is no time to call for your mummy, you wimp. Run!

Billy: *(Pointing)* No, look. It's a mummy!

Millie: Woah! You're right. It's covered in bandages and it's walking towards us. This is like something out of a horror film. Follow me!

(They exit, followed by the mummy)

Scene Two

A schoolroom in the desert. Miss Philips is talking to a class of mummies who are sitting at desks colouring in maps of Egypt

Miss Philips: So, we have found out how important the River Nile is. Who can tell us something about it?

(Meti puts her hand up)

Yes, Meti?

Meti: The wind pushes the sailboats one way, and the current takes them the other way, so it is easy to travel up and down on it.

Miss Philips: Well done, Bil- Meti. We haven't talked about that, how did you know? Did you read it in a book?

Meti: No, my mum told me. She had her own boat.

Ebio: *(Quietly)* Not bad for a mummy's boy.

Miss Philips: What was that, Mil- Ebio?

Ebio: Nothing, Miss. When can I show my scarab?

Miss Philips: Later. Ebio, I would like you and Meti to stay behind while the rest of the class goes to the temple. Off you go, everyone.

(The rest of the mummies file out)

Now, Ebio, I think you have something you need to say to Meti.

Ebio: No I don't. He's a wimp.

Meti: I'm not.

Ebio: You are, 'cos you're scared of the high priest.

Miss Philips: Ebio, anybody in their right mind is scared of the high priest. He brought you to life, and he could send you back to your tomb just as fast.

Ebio: What's all that dust outside?

Miss Philips: Don't try to change the subject.

Meti: No, she's right, Miss. There's lots of dust coming up as if people are running across the sand.

Miss Philips: I've told those mummies so many times not to run. If someone trips up and their bandages come undone, the results could be very nasty.

Ebio: It's coming from the other direction, Miss. The road from the temple.

Miss Philips: Hide, you two, quickly.

(They all hide under the desks. Billy and Millie run in)

Milly: Phew! I think we're far enough away now.

Billy: Yeah. Wow, this must be a school!

Millie: The desks are just like the ones at our school.

Billy: Yeah, so are the chairs!

Millie: And isn't that the box of pencils we packed for…?

(Miss Philips comes out from under a desk)

…Miss Philips!

Miss Philips: I told you not to rub that scarab. You must go back. You're in terrible danger.

Billy: What are you doing here?

Miss Philips: I'm teaching the mummies. I rubbed the scarab like you did and found myself here, and those poor mummies know nothing. I had to help them. I've been coming here for weeks. It's hard work but I really enjoy it.

Millie: So it is you who's been taking all the equipment from school?

Miss Philips: Yes, I'm afraid it is.

Millie: Cool!

Miss Philips: But you can't stay here. If the high priest finds you, he will use you for a sacrifice. He must not know you are here.

Billy: Um, he already does.

Miss Philips: What?

Billy: We saw him when we got here. He sent a mummy to chase us, that's why we were running and came here to hide.

Miss Philips: Oh no!

Millie: Is he in charge of the mummies?

Miss Philips: He found a way to bring them to life, but he can't do many at a time. He is training them to obey him. That's why I have to stay. The ones I teach are confident enough to say no to him. Of course he hates that, so he hates me, and if he could kill me he would. But he is afraid because he knows I have the power to leave and return. He thinks I go to the Afterlife.

Billy: Why does he think that?

Miss Philips: Because I told him.

Millie: You lied! Teachers should never lie!

Miss Philips: I had to. It was the only way to stay alive and get him to leave me alone. Look, you must go right now. You must run to the temple and find the door that you came through. Press the eye drawn on it and you will be taken safely back to school. Ebio and Meti will protect you on the way.

(Ebio and Meti stand up)

Ebio: Cool!

Meti: Do we have to?

(Billy and Millie hide under the desks)

Miss Philips: It's all right, you two. These are friendly mummies. Go now! Before it is too late!

Millie: I feel faint.

Miss Philips: Here, have some chocolate. And go! I must rush too as I'm late for the pharaoh, and he gets very grumpy if he is kept waiting. *(She leaves)*

Meti: Come on, let's get going.

Ebio: Hold on, chill out guys. We shouldn't go out into the open in daylight, so we'll take you somewhere safe and we can wait until it's safe to go to the temple.

Meti: Are you sure about this, Ebio?

Ebio: It will be fun. We can show them our new blue football kits.

Billy: I know where those came from – our school!

Ebio: Really? Thanks. My name means 'honey'. What does your name mean?

Millie: *(Looking confused)* Er… I don't know.

Billy: I do. Millie means 'honey'. I read it in a book.

Ebio: So our names are the same! We have to be friends!

(Exit)

Scene Three

The baker's house. The baker is mixing dough. His son Sabola is looking out of the window

Baker: Sabola, come here and help grind this corn.

Sabola: OK, Dad.

Baker: And make sure you do it properly: this bread is for the pharaoh.

Sabola: OK, Dad.

Baker: But make it fast because I'm in a hurry.

Sabola: OK, Dad.

Baker: And stop just saying 'OK Dad'.

Sabola: O–

(A ball comes through the window and lands in the dough. Millie appears at the window)

Millie: Ooops! Sorry. Can I have my ball back?

Baker: You've ruined this dough! It's full of dirt now!

Millie: It was an accident. Sorry.

Sabola: That's OK.

Millie: Thanks!

Baker: It is NOT OK! Sabola, stop saying OK to everyone and everything!

Sabola: OK.

Baker: Who are you, anyway? I've never seen you before.

Millie: I'm Millie. I only arrived today. And I'm going home tonight. In fact, I was on my way home when my friends said we should wait until it is dark before we go to the temple, so we stopped in their yard to play football and...

Sabola: What's football?

Millie: It's a game. Would you like to try it?

Sabola: Can I, Dad?

Baker: Oh, go on then. At least you said something apart from OK. I suppose you'll be needing this. *(He throws the ball to them)*

Millie: Thank you, Mister Baker. You are very kind! Now, Sabola isn't it? Yes. The first thing you need to know is that you use your feet to kick the ball and….

(They leave)

Baker: This is my lucky day. I heard there were strangers in town, and the high priest has put a reward on their heads. Messenger! Come here! It's urgent!

(Exits)

Scene Four

Billy, Millie, Ebio and Meti are at the temple

Millie: Tying those bandages together made a really good ball.

Billy: That was such a good game. Some of those mummies are great at football. Did you see me save that penalty, Millie? Of course you should never have given it, but I dived and just tipped it round the…

(High Priest enters with Mummy 1 and 2, and other mummies)

High Priest: Seize them!

(Mummies grab Millie and Billy. Ebio and Meti run away)

High Priest: Take this gold to the baker. He has earned it.

Mummy 1: Yes, master.

Millie: That rotten grumpy baker must have told on us.

Billy: You should have kept your big mouth shut.

Millie: What are you going to do with us?

High Priest: I have captured you, so you are my slaves. You will join my army of mummies and serve me.

You can help me find the secret of the Afterlife. I will use you in my next job – I'm going to be even more important.

Millie: *(Uncoils Sid from her arm)* Watch the snake. Watch the snake. Go to sleep. Go to sleep. When you wake up you will set us free and stop making an army of mummies and you'll just want to play football and…

High Priest: Nice try, dear, but I am a high priest and well used to such tricks. *(To the mummies)* Take them and guard them.

(Billie and Millie are led away by the mummies)

Billy: He's a nasty piece of work. It was brave of you to have a go at hypnotising him, Millie.

Millie: But it didn't work, did it?

Mummy 1: Can we play football now?

Mummy 2: Yes, can we?

Other guard mummies: Yes, please can we play now? What is it?

Millie: Well it didn't work on him, but it seems to have done the trick on them! It must only work with certain people!

Billy: OK you lot, we can play as much football as you like. We'll make a ball out of these bandages.

Guard mummies:	Hurray!
Billy:	*(To Millie)* We'll play football until it gets dark, and then escape back to the school, and we'll be safe.
Millie:	But what about Miss Philips?
Billy:	She's OK – she's friends with the pharaoh.
Millie:	But what if he isn't pharaoh for ever? What if that nasty priest gets to be pharaoh? He hates her. He'll kill her. Do you remember what we heard him say to that tall guy when we first arrived? About a plan being kept secret from the pharaoh?
Billy:	Oh yeah. That was the vizier. He's like a prime minister: the most important official who serves the pharaoh. They're plotting together. I bet they want to take power. If they do, Miss Philips will be in big trouble.
Mummies:	Football, football, football.
Millie:	OK, we need to play football with these mummies and then work out what to do. *(To mummies)* Come on guys, let's do some heading practice. Make sure those bandages are nice and tight. We don't want any accidents.

(They go off to play football)

Scene Five

Pharaoh, Vizier and Miss Philips are at the pharaoh's palace

Pharaoh: Owwww! It hurts!

Vizier: What's the matter, Your Majesty?

Pharaoh: Every time I eat anything my teeth hurt. Even a little piece of bread is agony! The gods are punishing me!

Miss Philips: Your Highness, I would be glad to bring some medicines from my country and cure your toothache.

Vizier: We have discussed this, Great Pharaoh. You know that we cannot trust this woman who appears and disappears. Ignore her, Your Majesty, and trust to our beliefs.

Pharaoh: Yes, I agree we cannot yet trust this woman or her medicines. We do not know her well enough. I am sorry, Misflips, you seem very nice but I have to be careful. There's always someone out to replace me. Owwwww!

Miss Philips: I understand you have to be careful, but you can trust me.

Vizier: Or can we? The high priest says you come from the Afterlife.

36

Pharaoh: What?

Miss Philips: Oh I just said that to him to frighten him, I didn't mean it.

Vizier: So you lied! You lied to our chief priest! You cannot trust this woman, Sire.

Pharaoh: But she is always nice to me. She brought that nice brown sweet stuff – what did you call it?

Miss Philips: Chocolate, Your Highness.

Vizier: It could be poison.

Pharaoh: Well I ate it and I'm still alive. It's soft and it doesn't hurt my teeth. But this bread does. Owwww!

Vizier: Shall I call the doctor?

Pharaoh: No! Last time he came I had to put crocodile dung on it. Yuck!

Miss Philips: Crocodile dung?!

Vizier: You know nothing of our customs, woman. Crocodile dung is a fine medicine with many uses.

Pharaoh: It tasted disgusting!

Vizier: The high priest said prayers over it so it had the blessing of the gods.

Pharaoh: Where is he? I need his help.

High Priest: *(Marches in)* Greetings, Sire, and greetings, Vizier. Oh, and are YOU still here?

Miss Philips: Yes, I've just been hearing about you blessing crocodile dung to put on the pharaoh's tooth. Very sensible, I'm sure.

High Priest: See how she distrusts our ways, Your Majesty? I believe she is an evil spirit who means us harm.

Pharaoh: Well she's always been very nice to me. Owwwww! And she says she can get medicines for my toothache. I think I might give it a try!

Vizier: No! No, Your Majesty. I believe the high priest has spoken with the gods and has a message about your toothache; have you not, High Priest?

High Priest: Indeed I have. The gods have spoken.

Miss Philips: What did they say then, these so-called gods?

Vizier: See how she mocks the very gods, Your Highness!

Pharaoh: Yes that was a bit rude, Misflips. And you are only a woman, after all.

High Priest: Your Majesty, I respectfully ask that this woman be taken from the room while I deliver the message from the gods. They told me not to speak it in front of her.

Pharaoh: Really? Owwww! Misflips, why don't you visit my zoo? You will see many animals which will be new to you I'm sure – we have a hippopotamus, a giraffe, and many lions!

Miss Philips: If Your Majesty wishes it, I will leave you to talk.

Pharaoh: Thanks very much!

(Miss Philips leaves)

She's ever so nice, you know.

Vizier: If you say so, Your Highness.

Pharaoh: Owwww! Right then, High Priest, what did the gods say?

High Priest: I have made offerings and said many prayers. I have had many conversations with the gods to make sure their answer is clear.

Pharaoh: Do get on with it. My teeth hurt.

High Priest: The gods have spoken. They say there is only one way to cure your toothache. It is to take Misflips to the altar.

Pharaoh: What, marry her? But I already have five wives! Oh well, if the gods insist, I suppose I could have another one.

High Priest: No no, Your Majesty misunderstands.

Pharaoh: Are you accusing me of being wrong? Remember, I am a deity.

Vizier: No no, I'm sure that is not what the high priest is saying. He is saying that he did not express himself clearly enough. Try again, High Priest, and make it clearer.

High Priest: The gods have spoken. The only way to cure your toothache is to take Misflips to the altar and sacrifice her.

Pharaoh: Sacrifice her? I thought we only did that with enemy soldiers we capture in battle?

High Priest: The problem is so difficult that only this sacrifice will cure it.

Pharaoh: And that is what the gods said?

High Priest: The gods have spoken.

Pharaoh: Well, if the gods have spoken, we'd better do it. What a shame. Guards! Take Misflips to her room and keep her there. Owww! This pesky tooth hurts!

Exit

Scene Six

Miss Philips' room. Messenger enters with Miss Philips

Miss Philips: What? Could you say that again?

Messenger: The pharaoh asks that you stay in your room.

Miss Philips: But he's not asking, if there are guards at the door. He's telling me. What's going to happen to me?

Messenger: I heard them say that you are to be taken to the altar.

Miss Philips: Wow! Does he want to marry me?

Messenger: Um. No. We don't use an altar for the pharaoh's marriages. At least, I'm sure we didn't for the first five.

Miss Philips: Oh. Let me guess. This was a message from the gods, wasn't it?

Messenger: Yes.

Miss Philips: And they sent it through the high priest.

Messenger: Of course. That is the way.

(Sabola enters with some bread)

Miss Philips: Then I am to die. There is no one here who can help me.

Messenger: I'm sorry. There is nothing I can do. *(Leaves)*

Miss Philips: Oh no. This is terrible. No one can help me now.

Sabola: Your friends can.

Miss Philips: I have no friends here, apart from the mummies I teach. And they can do nothing.

Sabola: I mean your friends from your own world.

Miss Philips: Millie and Billy? You've met them?

Sabola: Yes. They showed me how to play football.

Miss Philips: Before they went back?

Sabola: Yes, but the high priest captured them. He told his mummies to guard them but they made friends and now they are all playing football together. Billy is in goal. He's good at catching but he can be a bit slow to dive so if you shoot low you are more likely to score. It's worth aiming at the far post to–

Miss Philips: Playing football with his mummies? So they haven't gone yet?

Sabola: No, they're waiting for darkness. Oh this is terrible. Misflips, I see you are in trouble and I want to help. I blame my family for the capture of your friends. It was my father who told the high priest of their plans. He needed the money.

Miss Philips: I understand. Thank you for offering to help. Can you take a message for me?

Sabola: I'll have to hurry. It's getting dark.

Miss Philips: (*Writes quickly on a piece of papyrus*) Here, take this message to them and hurry!

Sabola: I'll go faster than grain falling from a sack!

(*Exit*)

Scene Seven

At the temple. Millie, Billy, Ebio and Meti are lurking in the shadows

Millie: We've made it to the temple. Watch out: there are people working here, but no one will see us if we stay in the shadows.

Billy: They must be preparing for a ceremony.

Millie: Shall we stay and watch?

Billy: We'd better not. It's dangerous for us here. The high priest might catch us and not all those mummies are as friendly as the ones you hypnotised.

Millie: Goodbye, Ebio. Thank you for your help.

Ebio: It is my pleasure.

Billy: Goodbye, Meti.

44

Meti: Goodbye, Billy. Can I just say that you need to dive a little earlier for low shots – those were the only kind you let in in the game.

Billy: Thanks!

Sabola: *(Runs in, shouting)* Stop!

Ebio: Run, it's the baker's son. He will betray us!

Sabola: No, stop. I'm a friend. I have a letter from Misflips.

Billy: Give it to me. *(Reads)* Dear Millie and Billy. You are in terrible danger. I am to be sacrificed to cure the pharaoh's toothache. I don't think it will be long before the high priest does the same to you. Go back to your world and never return. Goodbye and good luck.

Millie: Sacrificed?

Sabola: Yes. It is the will of the gods.

High Priest: *(In the distance, on the other side of the temple)* Hurry up, get that knife sharper! Light more fires! The ceremony is to be held soon! Who's that over there?

Ebio: Go. Go to your world now or you will be killed too.

(Billy and Millie put their hands on the eye)

Act Three Scene One

They fall into classroom, next to the Ancient Egypt display

Millie: Did that really happen?

Billy: My shoes and pockets are full of sand, so I think it did.

Millie: I'll check my pockets. Ooh, it's the chocolate that Miss Philips gave me!

Mr Sweet: *(Enters)* Ha! Caught you red handed! I saw you sneak out of assembly and I followed you. You are the chocolate thief! Go to my room right now.

Millie: *(Produces her snake)* Watch the snake. Watch the snake. Go to sleep. Go to sleep. When you wake up you won't remember where you found the chocolate. You won't like sweet things any more, and um…

(Billy whispers something in her ear)

…you will decide that break times will be twice as long, and the school will ban all homework.

(Mr Sweet stands still, staring into space)

Billy: Let's give him a gentle push into the stock room, so no one finds him. There.

Millie: Poor Miss Philips must be dead by now. Oh, I wish we could have saved her.

Billy: Don't you see? We still can. It's the same time now as it was when we left: Mr Sweet has just come out of assembly. No time has passed here at all. Maybe that means no time will pass in Egypt while we work out what to do.

Millie: Brilliant! So, how are we going to save her?

Billy: Could we get the friendly mummies to do it?

Millie: There aren't enough of them, and there are still loads who are loyal to the high priest.

Billy: Could you hypnotise them while we get her out?

Millie: I couldn't hypnotise them all, and remember it didn't work on the high priest, so it's too risky.

Billy: Hang on a minute. Why are they going to sacrifice Miss Philips?

Millie: Let's look at the letter again. It was to cure the pharaoh's toothache. That might just be an excuse made up by the high priest, but if we could cure his toothache, he won't have a reason to sacrifice her, will he?

Billy: We could take medicines back.

Millie: I bet Miss Philips would have suggested that,

too. But I bet they wouldn't trust her enough to use them.

(They hear the sound of pupils going to class)

Billy: Look, people will be suspicious if they don't see you around. I'm new and I won't be missed yet. You go off to class and I'll try to find a cure they would understand. We've got all these books right here on the display.

Millie: Good thinking, Billy.

(Millie leaves just as Raki comes in)

Raki: Hi Billy. What are you doing? You're supposed to be in the cookery lesson.

Billy: I'm trying to find out why the pharaoh has a toothache.

Raki: You what?

Billy: Er, sorry, I was talking rubbish. I'm trying to work out why an Ancient Egyptian's teeth would hurt. It's for our topic.

Raki: Can I help? I hate cooking so I said I had to go and wash my hands again. That's the third time! I'll look in the books with you.

Billy: OK.

48

(They flick through the books)

Raki: Found anything yet?

Billy: Only something about crocodile dung, and I don't think anyone would be stupid enough to fall for that.

Raki: Look, this is weird. This is the skeleton of some ancient pharaoh, and the caption says his teeth were nearly worn out.

Billy: Let me see. *(Reads)* 'Their teeth were ground down by little bits of grit and sand that got into their bread.'

Raki: Huh, they should have used a sieve.

Billy: What?

Raki: If you put stuff through a sieve, the bigger bits get caught and only the tiniest pieces, like flour, get through. We've just been using them in cookery.

Billy: Raki, can you do me a favour? Go and get Millie. Tell her to sneak out and tell her to bring a sieve.

Raki: A sieve? What do you want a sieve for?

Billy: I can't tell you but it's a matter of life and death!

Raki: OK, I'm going.

(Raki runs off, and Millie soon returns with the sieve)

Millie: How is the sieve going to help?

Billy: I'll tell you on the way. Bring the sieve, and try to think if we met a baker in Egypt.

Millie: *(Voice fading as Billy rubs the scarab)* Oh yes: Sabola's dad. But I bet he won't help….

Scene Two

The bakery in Ancient Egypt

Baker: Sabola, come here and help grind this corn.

Sabola: OK, Dad.

Baker: And make sure you do it properly: this bread is for the pharaoh.

Sabola: OK, Dad.

Baker: But make it fast because I'm in a hurry – I need to take this up for the feast after the sacrifice.

Sabola: OK, Dad.

Baker: And stop just saying 'OK, Dad'.

Sabola: O–

(A sieve comes through the window and lands in the dough. Millie appears at the window)

Baker: *(Scared)* Oh no, the ghost of that girl has come to get revenge. Please don't harm me, I'm sorry!

Millie: Well, Mister Baker, I can't say it was very nice of you to tell the high priest where we were. But I escaped, so we're quits. I will forgive you if you to do me a little favour.

Baker: What? I'll do anything. Just tell me.

Millie: Is that the bread for the pharaoh's feast?

Baker: Yes. Do you want me to put poison in it?

Millie: No! But pass the flour through this sieve before you make it into bread. OK?

Baker: OK. *(Shakes his head)* Now even I'm saying OK as well. Come on, Sabola, we have work to do.

Sabola: Yes, Sir! I mean, OK, Dad.

(Exit)

Scene Three

The High Priest, Vizier, Pharaoh and mummies are in the temple

High Priest: The gods have spoken.

All: The gods have spoken.

High Priest: We know the cure for the pharaoh's toothache.

All: We know the cure for the pharaoh's toothache.

High Priest: Misflips must be sacrificed.

All: Misflips must be sacrificed.

High Priest: The gods have spoken.

All: The gods have spoken.

Pharaoh: Now you are sure about this, aren't you, High Priest? It's not going to be a flop like that crocodile dung? Owww!

High Priest: The gods have spoken.

Pharaoh: Look, you can stop saying that. Oww! We all know that the gods have spoken.

All: The gods have spoken.

Pharaoh: Silence! That's better. You can't hear yourself think round here. Right, we'd better get it over with. Bring in Misflips.

(Miss Philips is brought in by two mummy guards)

Those are rather creepy-looking guards. What happened to the other ones?

Vizier: They refused to do the job, Sir.

Pharaoh: Refused?

Vizier: Yes, Sire. They will be punished soon.

Pharaoh: But why did they refuse?

Vizier: It seems Misflips has been teaching some of the mummies and they have become loyal to her. This shows that she is a threat to your power, Sire, and this is all the more reason to sacrifice her.

Pharaoh: Well I'm not surprised she's popular. She's very nice. But if the gods have spoken. DON'T ANYBODY REPEAT THAT! If the gods have spoken, that's it, isn't it?

High Priest: Bring Misflips to the altar and hand me the knife. Now is the moment to end the great suffering of the pharaoh. *(He raises the knife)*

(Billy and Millie rush in)

Billy: Stop!

Millie: Stop the sacrifice!

High Priest: What is this? Guards, take them away!

Millie: Oh, hello guards. We haven't met before, have we, but I bet you've spoken to your friends who play football with me?

Mummy: Yes, we have.

Millie: Would you like to play now?

Mummy: We're supposed to help here.

Millie: *(Removes Sid the snake from her sleeve)* Watch the snake. Watch the snake. You want to play football and practise banana shots round a pyramid. Follow me.

(The mummies follow her out of the temple)

Billy: Pharaoh, I can show you why you have toothache. I can cure your toothache – in fact I can stop teeth from hurting across your whole kingdom!

Vizier: Do not listen, Sire. This is a plot.

Billy: And you know all about plots, don't you? You and the high priest, with his army of mummies, have your own plans, don't you?

(Vizier and High Priest look at each other guiltily. Everybody stares at them and starts mumbling about them plotting)

Pharaoh: Silence! Misflips, is this a friend of yours?

Miss Philips: I haven't known him long, but I would trust him with my life, Sire.

Pharaoh: Very well. We will hear what he has to say. Tell me why my teeth hurt.

Billy: It's because of the bread.

High Priest: Bread! What rubbish! Why are you listening to this child when the gods have already spoken?

Pharaoh: Go on, young one.

Billy: Your bread has got little bits of grit and sand in it. When you eat it, this rubs against your teeth and that is why they hurt.

Pharaoh: If the bread is at fault, it is the baker who will be hurt. Bring me the baker.

Millie: He's coming. We showed him how to stop getting grit and sand in the bread, and he's going to bring you a loaf. As soon as you eat it, we will know who is right.

Pharaoh: These are clever young ones. You have done well, Misflips!

Miss Philips: Thank you.

(The baker arrives with Millie and the mummies)

Baker: Greetings, Your Majesty, and to all these noble people. May I say what an honour it is to…

Pharaoh: Never mind all that. Bring me the loaf.

Billy: Let's hope it's not a sandwich.

Miss Philips: If we get out of this alive, Billy, we must do something about improving your jokes.

Pharaoh: Tasty bread, Baker…

(They silently watch him chew the bread)

Hmm. That is good. No pain!

Miss Philips: Phew!

Billy: Phew!

Millie: Phew!

High Priest: Phooey. I'm off. I'm not hanging around in a country where kids run the show.

Pharaoh: Not so fast, High Priest. You as well, Vizier. The boy was right about the bread. I wonder if he is right about the plot, too. Guards, seize them and tie them up.

(The guards look at Millie, who nods. They tie up the High Priest and the Vizier)

Pharaoh: So I can eat bread whenever I like?

Miss Philips: Yes.

Pharaoh: And my teeth won't hurt?

Miss Philips: Well, they might hurt a bit but they should feel better.

Pharaoh: That is an honest and sensible answer. I would be mad to sacrifice you. But I would still like to take you to the altar.

Miss Philips: You mean…?

Pharaoh: Marry me, Misflips. Be one of my wives!

Miss Philips: Well, I'll have to think about it.

Pharaoh: I am the pharaoh! I decide, not you!

Miss Philips: But where I come from, women decide as well. I'll let you know.

Pharaoh: What a strange, uncivilised place that must be. All right, let me know by dusk tomorrow.

(Exit)

Scene Four

Meti, Ebio, Miss Philips, Millie and Billy are in the mummies' schoolroom

Miss Philips: So I have to decide. Stay, or go. I can't keep switching between the modern world and here, it gets too confusing.

Millie: It's nearly time to tell the pharaoh. Are you coming back with us, or staying here?

Miss Philips: Billy, what was it you told the class about boats on the Nile?

Billy: The wind blows them one way…

Meti: And the current takes them the other.

Miss Philips: So they just cruise up and down the river. Do you know, after years of teaching in a 21st-century school that sounds like a very nice way to live. And the pharaoh is very kind when you get to know him, and no one will plot against him after he has made an example of the high priest and the vizier. And do you know it never rains in Egypt? Not ever! I have made my decision. Children: would you like to see an Ancient Egyptian wedding before you go?

Millie: Yes, please!

(Exit)

Scene Five

*The school the next day. Millie and Billy are
dressed as mummies*

Millie: What an adventure!

Billy: Yesterday was the best first day at school anyone
could have.

Millie: Yeah, it was pretty good, wasn't it? Mind you, it
almost feels like a dream now. I feel as if none
of it happened.

Billy: Hang on, we forgot something yesterday: we
didn't wake up Mr Sweet!

Millie: Oooops.

*(They rush to the stock cupboard. Millie clicks her
fingers in front of Mr Sweet. He wakes up)*

Mr Sweet: Hello, you two. Excellent costumes! Pay your
money then. Jolly good. Off you go to enjoy a
nice long game of football – double break times
from now on. And I must remember to write a
newsletter and tell everyone that all homework
is cancelled.

*(Millie and Billy run out but stop at edge of stage
when they hear Mr Sweet say the words...)*

Mr Sweet: *(To Ebio and Meti, who have entered)* Hello, you two. Excellent costumes! Pay your money then. Jolly good. Off you go to enjoy a nice long game of football.

Millie: Wow, he's in a good mood.

Billy: Yes, but who's he talking to? There was no one there. Have I sent him completely crazy?

(Two more mummies appear)

Mr Sweet: Hello, you two. Excellent costumes! Pay your money then. Jolly good. Off you go to enjoy a nice long game of football.

Millie: Are you thinking what I'm thinking?

Billy: What are you thinking?

Millie: I'm wondering if we shut that door properly behind us.

Billy: Miss Philips is bound to stop them soon.

(They go back into the room. There are four mummies doing warm-ups and Mr Sweet is staring at his hand)

Mr Sweet: This is gold! Pure gold! We can use this to buy all the equipment we need! We can even have a bowl of fruit in every classroom and the staffroom! Yippee! *(He runs off)*

Millie:	Hello, Ebio.
Ebio:	Hello, Millie.
Billy:	Hello, Meti.
Meti:	Hello, Billy.
Millie:	And you bought some friends with you. Well you look all set for a game of football. Let's play!

(All exit)

Scene Six

We are in the middle of a football match between two schools. Billy's mum is watching from the sidelines, next to Mr Sweet. Mr Flinton blows his whistle

Mr Flinton:	Penalty!
Millie:	It was an accident, ref!
Mr Flinton:	Millie, as team captain you are allowed to speak to me, but you must admit that when one of your players swings his bandage round his head and lassoes an opponent, that is a foul.
Millie:	Er, well I think his arm was falling off.

Mr Flinton: You assured me at the start of this game that the unusual kit some of your players are wearing was because they had been hurt on the way to school. They are covered in bandages. Now you are telling me they are falling apart? I'm starting to wonder if I was right to allow them to play at all.

Millie: No, no, you're quite right, Mr Flinton. Just a sec, though… Team, gather round for a moment. That's it. Round Mr Flinton. *(Brings out Sid the snake)* Watch the snake. Watch the snake. You are feeling sleepy. When you wake up you will think it is perfectly normal for footballers to wear bandages all over their bodies.

(She clicks her fingers. Mr Flinton wakes up and blows his whistle)

Great save, Billy! Pass to me!

Mrs Taylor: *(To Mr Sweet on the touchline)* Billy seems very settled at this school – I really didn't need to worry. And he has learned so much about Ancient Egypt! It's almost as if he's been there! Oh good goal, Millie!

(The End)

EXPLORING THE PLAY

Act One Scene One

Hotseating

Hotseat Billy about how he feels on his first day at his new school. Choose one member of the class to be Billy – he/she is in the hotseat. Ask him or her, in character, questions. How does he get on with his mother? Why does he tell her she need not come in? How does he feel about Sid the snake?

Freeze-framing

Freeze-frame the moment when Millie produces Sid the snake from her sleeve. Talk about the different reactions people have to snakes and show how these would be revealed in their expressions.

Scene Two

Writing

What is Mr Sweet like? How do you know? Write a paragraph describing his character. Why do you think the author gave him this name?

Scene Three

Improvisation

In this scene Ishrak is hypnotised. We see in scene 5 that he thinks he remembers what happened but can't put it into words. Imagine what it feels like to be hypnotised and to wake up afterwards. Write his 'internal dialogue' – what he says to himself as he goes through this process, and as he tries to answer Mr Sweet in scene 5.

Scene Four

Writing

Use books and the Internet to investigate Egyptian beliefs in the Afterlife and scarabs. Write a short report on the objects people were buried with and what they thought happened after death.

Acting

Billie and Millie do not trust or like each other much. In pairs, act out how they would react to each other. Start by just using their expressions and bodies. Then add words to the characterisation.

Scene Five

Mime

The assembly started with the wrong, very loud, music being played. Then Mr Sweet listed all the things that had been taken. He announced the fancy dress day and finally that break times would be cancelled. How would people have looked as they reacted to these things? Try to use your whole body as well as your face.

Scene Six

Staging

How would you stage this scene to show the children being taken away on a journey through time? What sound effects would you use? Have some actors moving backwards or perhaps flying in slow motion. What might they see on their journey?

Act Two Scene One

Tableaux

Think of what you would see in ancient Egypt – things such as pyramids, the Sphinx, camels and the desert. In groups, make shapes to create a picture, or tableau, of these scenes. Make them come to life and freeze at the click of a finger.

Improvisation

The high priest and the vizier are clearly plotting something. How would their faces and bodies show this? One way that people who are co-operating act is to use echo-gestures, where they copy each other's expressions and movements. In pairs, sit or stand opposite each other and improvise a conversation. Use movement to show that you are plotting something.

Scene Two

Writing

How does the author suggest that Ebio and Meti are like Millie and Billy? List the ways in which this is done. If you were staging the play, how could you show this physically, too? Write a sentence or two explaining your ideas.

Improvisation

The high priest has found a way to bring mummies to life, but he can only do a few at a time, so it must be quite complicated. Improvise a scene where he does this – try it with and without words, just with movement. Act out how the mummies are 'activated' and how they react.

Drawing

Design a costume for the mummies in which they can still move about and play football. What materials would you use?

Scene Three

Improvisation

At the start of the scene Sabola says the same words every time he speaks. Set a scene with two or three characters in which one uses the same word or phrase all the time. How do the other characters react?

Scene Four

Writing and drawing

How would you explain the rules of football, or another game, to someone who has never played it before? What would you say? How would you use your body? Write and draw what you would say and do.

Scene Five

Word game

The Egyptian characters refer to Miss Philips as Misflips because they hear her name as one sound. Play a game where you name a person or object in a similar way. Can the other people guess what you are referring to?

Scene Six

Hot-seating

How do Miss Philips' feelings change through this scene? Ask her what she was thinking at different points in it. What are her feelings about the pharaoh?

Drawing

What do you think the sacrifice scene should look like? Where would you put the characters? Make a sketch of this. What colours would you use to add to the effect?

Act Three Scene One

Improvisation

Raki finds an excuse to leave the cookery lesson. In pairs, act out a role-play, with a pupil making up excuses to get out of the room, and a teacher answering each excuse with a way to keep the child where they are.

Scene Two

Mime

The baker thinks he is seeing Millie's ghost. How would he react? Use your body to show how you might react to seeing
• a ghost
• a monster

• a crying baby
• a robber
• an angel

Scene Three

Mime

Billy reveals he knows the vizier and high priest have been plotting. How would the other people in the room react? Would the pharaoh behave differently to one of his slaves? Mime the expressions of the other people in the scene.

Scene Four

Writing

Miss Philips has to decide whether to stay in Ancient Egypt or return to the modern world. Use what she says and your own imagination to write a list of pros and cons. If it was your choice, what would you do?

Scene Five

Movement

How would you show that a mummy is friendly, even if it looks really scary? Practise walking about in the classic mummy pose with arms outstretched, showing different characteristics such as friendly, scared, threatening, excited and sad.

Scene Six

The play ends with a football match. In groups, create a tableau showing an event in a football game or the reaction of the crowd. Show it to the rest of the class and see if they can guess what is happening.